Judi -
Get well
soon!!
Love, Lisa

The Secret Remedy Book

A STORY OF COMFORT AND LOVE

By Karin Cates

Illustrated by Wendy Anderson Halperin

ORCHARD BOOKS

An Imprint of Scholastic Inc. ✦ New York

To my husband, Lloyd Cates
—K. C.

Dedicated to the remedies . . .
the simple acts of making things better.
—W. A. H.

◆ ◆ ◆

Text copyright © 2003 by Karin Cates
Illustrations copyright © 2003 by Wendy Anderson Halperin
Library of Congress Cataloging-in-Publication Data available.
ISBN 0-439-35226-6
10 9 8 7 6 5 4 3 2 1   03 04 05 06 07
Printed in Mexico   49
First Scholastic edition, June 2003
The text type is set in 13-point Bernhard Modern.
Hand-lettering is by David Coulson.

Lolly's family visited Auntie Zep on every holiday. Auntie Zep always had a bonfire or a pet rabbit or a secret in the attic to make the visits exciting. Lolly often wished that she could visit her Auntie by herself. One summer, Mother and Father decided that Lolly was old enough to stay with Auntie Zep for a whole month. At last! Lolly could hardly wait!

But after her family dropped her off, Lolly found that she felt a little sad. She tried to make the sad feeling go away, but she only got sadder and sadder. And before she could stop herself, she sat down and cried.

Auntie Zep wiped away Lolly's tears and said, "We need to get *The Secret Remedy Book*."

First, they had to locate the key to the trunk where the book was kept. Auntie Zep knew just where to find it.

Then Auntie Zep took Lolly to the attic to find the trunk, which was very old. It had both a watery smell like the ocean and a sun-dried smell like the desert, for the trunk had once traveled far and wide.

Lolly turned the key in the lock until they heard a little clicking sound. Auntie Zep helped Lolly open the heavy lid. The smell of mothballs rushed out of the trunk like a cold wind. There it was! *The Secret Remedy Book*.

The remedy book was covered with an old piece of
flowery wallpaper. The pages were brown, brittle, and
raggedy, and dried flowers were pressed between some
of them. There were splotches here and there where
something had spilled or splattered onto the paper.

Very carefully, Lolly turned the pages. The remedies were written in a spidery handwriting that seemed to scuttle and scurry across each page. Lolly thought the writing looked as if it were in a hurry to help her feel better. She drew in her breath when she read the words on the first page:

Warning!

*You must finish all the remedies in
this book before the first hoot of an owl —
or none of them will work!*

The First Remedy

Drink one glass of apple juice.
You must drink it so carefully that you can almost taste the
very apple tree that made the apples that made the juice.

Lolly and Auntie Zep each drank a glass of fresh apple juice.
Auntie said that she could almost taste the leaves of the apple tree.
Lolly said that she could almost taste the blossoms.

Closing their eyes, they felt almost as if they were in the
very orchard where the tree grew.

"What about the owl?" asked Lolly.

"Oh, we have hours before the owl hoots," said Auntie Zep.

The Second Remedy

Plant a seed in good earth.
You must do something sneaky to keep the seed safe.

Lolly and Auntie Zep buried a handful of pumpkin
seeds in the dark, rich mounds of earth in Auntie's
garden. Then they made a scarecrow, complete with a
floppy hat, a flowery dress, and a necklace of cans.

The dress flapped furiously in the wind; the cans clattered and clanked.

Lolly took Auntie Zep's hand. "Let's run back and see what the next remedy will be."

The Third Remedy

Take a walk as far as you can.
You must see something that you
have never noticed before.

Lolly and Auntie Zep hurried down a footpath through the woods. They looked and looked for something they had never noticed before. All at once, there it was! A piece of railroad track lay partly buried. Both ends of the track disappeared into the earth, as mysteriously as a rainbow.

"When will an owl hoot?" Lolly asked, as soon as they were back at Auntie Zep's.

"We have plenty of time," she replied.

The Fourth Remedy

Feed a wild thing.
You must make a solemn promise that you will always do
everything you can to protect it from hunger and harm.

In the kitchen, Auntie Zep fed Lolly, saying that Lolly was a wild thing! The big sandwich disappeared munch by munch and the cool, sweet apple vanished crunch by crunch with barely a crust and a core and a lettuce leaf left behind.

Then Lolly took a pail of leftovers outside to a burrow in which an opossum lived. "I solemnly promise," Lolly said into the dark burrow, "that I will always do everything I can to protect you from hunger and harm."

The Fifth Remedy

Write a cheerful letter to some dear soul.
You must put something unexpected
in the envelope.

Auntie Zep wrote to Lolly's mother.
"I'll write to Father," Lolly said.
Auntie Zep put a heart-shaped leaf in her letter.
Lolly put a mockingbird's feather in hers.

"Will an owl hoot now?" Lolly asked as she sealed her envelope.

"Soon," said Auntie Zep.

So Lolly hurried to turn another brown, crackling page of *The Secret Remedy Book*.

The Sixth Remedy

Read in peace and quiet from a favorite book.
You must find one special part of the book that is so
wonderful that you feel like reading it again and again.

Lolly leaped into the comfy, four-poster bed. She opened
a poetry book that had a little ribbon in it for marking your
place. Pretty soon she had learned a poem by heart. The poem
was short, but the words were bigger than the whole night.
Auntie Zep said that poetry was like that sometimes.

Lolly was getting very sleepy. "Did you hear an owl hoot?" she whispered.

"Not yet," said Auntie Zep. "We still have time for the very last remedy."

The Seventh Remedy

Dream of doing great things. You must think of one small, great thing you can do tomorrow.

Lolly said that tomorrow she would write her very own poem. Then she began to slip into a comfortable dreaminess.

She dreamed about saving all the wild things and
planting forests and writing poetry. She dreamed about
sleeping in a tent. There were so many things to do!

Auntie Zep had a deep, dreamy look on her face, too. She dreamed about climbing mountains and taking Lolly to see all the beauty of the world someday.

Suddenly they heard the soft, trembling hoot of an owl in the darkness outside the window.

"Did *The Secret Remedy Book* work for you?" Auntie Zep whispered as she closed the book, tucked the covers around Lolly, and kissed her forehead.

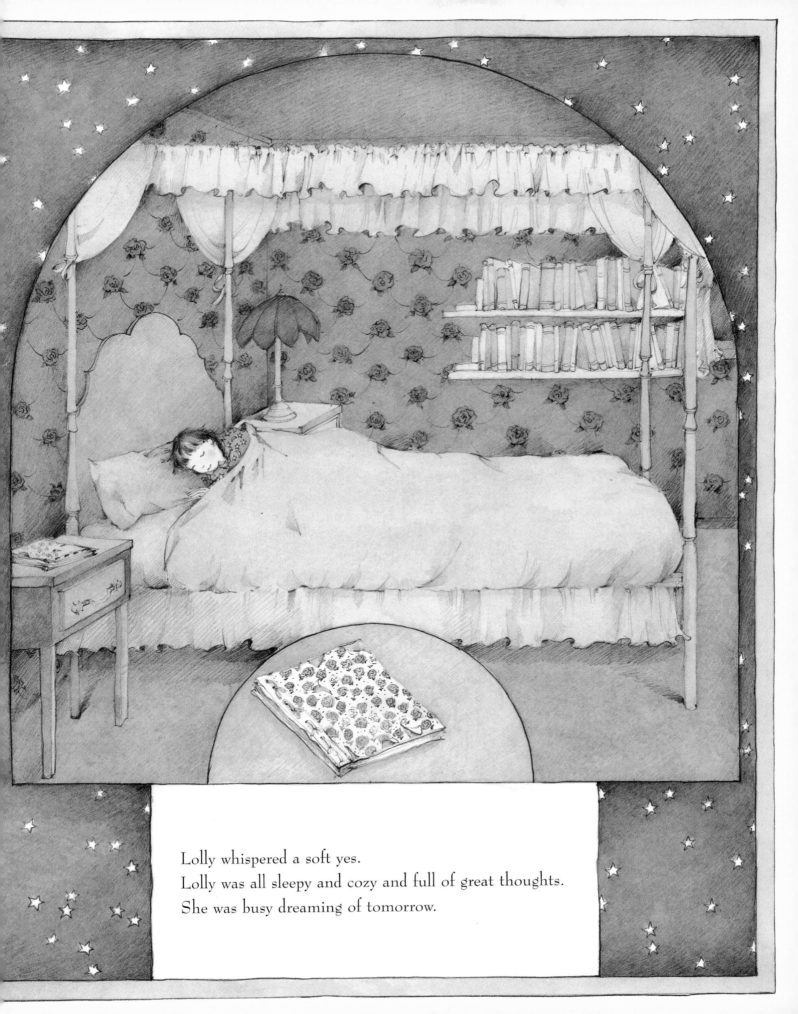

Lolly whispered a soft yes.
Lolly was all sleepy and cozy and full of great thoughts.
She was busy dreaming of tomorrow.

The Secret Remedies

1. Drink one glass of apple juice.
You must drink it so carefully that you can almost taste the
very apple tree that made the apples that made the juice.

2. Plant a seed in good earth.
You must do something sneaky to keep the seed safe.

3. Take a walk as far as you can.
You must see something that you have never noticed before.

4. Feed a wild thing.
You must make a solemn promise that you will always do
everything you can to protect it from hunger and harm.

5. Write a cheerful letter to some dear soul.
You must put something unexpected in the envelope.

6. Read in peace and quiet from a favorite book.
You must find one special part of the book that is so
wonderful that you feel like reading it again and again.

7. Dream of doing great things.
You must think of one small, great thing
you can do tomorrow.